I0731095

ARIZONA LEGEND

A Western Adventure

A.T. BUTLER

Jacob Payne fished his worn billfold out of his jacket pocket and set it on the bank countertop. It was fat and full, jam-packed with greenbacks, and sat next to his larger leather pouch. This was the same pouch that, until that morning, had been stored at the bottom of his saddlebag for months. The tall, broad-shouldered bounty hunter waited patiently while the meek man opposite him figured out what to do.

Jacob had come to the Liberty Trust Bank first thing that November morning, the smell of coffee still on his breath. Now that he had finally made a decision, he knew he shouldn't put it off any longer. The dollar bills had just been piling up unspent, waiting for a purpose. The bounty hunter had stashed away all the cash made from various hunts and jobs for about nine months already. It was time he actually did something with it.

The thin young man behind the bank counter, who kept compulsively pushing his wispy long blond hair out of his face, took in the sight. He nervously chewed on his thumbnail, while Jacob waited.

"And all this is to be deposited in your new account, Mr. Payne?" the bank teller asked, visibly surprised. "That is... uh. You need a new account, sir? Please wait here, sir. Thank you, sir. I think the manager would prefer that he help you personally."

Jacob nodded, turned to look out the bank's big front windows as the young man bustled away to find someone else. The Tucson Mountains could be seen in the distance, over the roofs of the shops across the street. The rough, jagged peaks still bereft of snow put Jacob in mind of the rough, rugged days he had on his way to this new life he was leading. Weeks on the road, never knowing when he'd get to sleep or where he'd get his next meal.

When Jacob had come west to the Arizona Territory at the start of that year, he had been running away from his past. It certainly had not been an easy path to run. It was a common story, one shared with many other men in the harsh wilderness west of the Mississippi. Why else would so many men and women choose to go without the luxuries and technology of more established cities? Without the safety of a reliable law? These men knew what they were choosing when they hit the open road.

No, like so many other migrants, Jacob had been willing to sacrifice certain comforts just for the benefit of avoiding others. Specifically his family, his brothers, and the draining responsibility that all represented. He had spent his entire life to that point trying to live up to what they expected of him. But after his wife Louisa had died, he was tired. Tired of being beholden and tired of living for someone else's wishes.

And so he had run. He could admit that now. Jacob was running away from his old life in the east, not thinking about what he was running toward. At the time it didn't matter. He just needed to get out.

Jacob had arrived in Tucson in January of that year, and immediately began seeking his fortune as a bounty hunter, tracking down the bank robbers, murderers, rapists and snake oil salesmen that had also come to the frontier. He had been unsurprised to find himself quite good at his new chosen vocation. Jacob had the skills necessary for tracking, and the moral fortitude necessary to stay on the right side of the law. He was strong in body and mind, exactly what was needed in a man of his work.

But because he didn't have a plan, all he had done over the previous months was hoard the hundreds of dollars he had earned. Little by little he had squirreled it away. Twenty dollars. Fifty. Soon he was commanding bounties of one hundred dollars and more. But other than his room and board, and maybe a few small losses at the poker table, Jacob didn't have anything to spend his money on.

He had had a vague idea of returning to Virginia one day, to buy the family estate out from under his brother. Each time Jacob added to his savings he imagined his brother's shocked face. In the right person's hands, spite could be a very motivating emotion. But the longer he was in Arizona, the more the sting went out of his memories. Jacob couldn't make any more big, life-altering decisions just based on vindictiveness. The slights and insults he had suffered became the wounds of schoolchildren. The power of reclaiming the family plantation became the goal of a self-centered man.

The longer Jacob lived in the western territories, the more he realized that anything he returned to in the States would feel hollow and tame compared to what he had now. Though it had its drawbacks, being a bounty hunter in Arizona was where he needed to be.

And so he kept saving, but without any aim. Another hundred. Two hundred. More and more he stashed away the cash that he earned. The Widows and Orphans Fund of Tucson received a few anonymous donations, but for the most part Jacob was at a loss for how else to spend his money.

But now that he was staying in Tucson for the most extended period he had up till that point, Jacob figured it was high time he acted responsible about all this, and at the very least, not leave himself open to risk. Sitting on literal bags of cash was the act of a fool.

"Mr. Payne?"

Jacob broke out of his reminiscing, and turned back around to find himself facing a small round man with a fastidious mustache and red checkered bow tie. The sight of him on the other side of the counter took Jacob aback for a short moment—he couldn't recall having seen a bow tie since getting west of Austin. Though, to be fair, most men he knew would eschew collars as well if they could get away with it. He shook off his surprise and smiled at the bank manager.

"Yes, sir. Thank you mighty for your help with this."

"Of course, sir." The manager eyed the stacks of cash on the counter in front of him, though Jacob could tell he was trying not to be obvious. "My name is Mr. Bagley. I've been the manager of Liberty Trust Bank for five years now. Since the town was very first founded."

"Impressive," Jacob said, nodding.

"You're in good hands, Mr. Payne." He looked immensely pleased with himself. "You'd like to deposit all of this, I understand?"

"Yes. Please. I'll need a new account, of course. And I think you can expect me to deposit more every week or so, depending on how business is."

"Ah, yes." Mr. Bagley chuckled. "And as I understand it, your business is booming."

Jacob didn't return the laugh. "Unfortunately, yes. That is the case."

Mr. Bagley cleared his throat awkwardly.

"I aim to do my job well enough to put myself out of business," Jacob continued.

"Yes ... well." The bank manager nodded fervently. "I quite understand. All the more reason to keep these earnings safe and secure in the Liberty Trust Bank."

Jacob smiled. "Thank you."

Mr. Bagley picked up Jacob's billfold and pouch off the counter and indicated the bounty hunter should follow him. "Come back to my office, Mr. Payne. I'll get the paperwork started and you'll be set."

There was only one other customer in the bank at that early hour. Mr. Bart, the pharmacist, nodded to Jacob as he passed.

"Mr. Bart," Jacob said, tipping his hat. "I hope your wife is well."

"She is. Thank you, sir."

The last time Jacob had seen Mrs. Bart, she had been sitting in the dust on the boardwalk outside their shop, sobbing as a team of men from the Slippery Stone Gang mangled and looted. Though bringing the gang to Tucson had not exactly been Jacob's fault, his involvement with the entire debacle weighed heavily on him. He couldn't have stopped the pharmacy from being destroyed any more than he had been able to stop the gang from demolishing the school, the dry goods store and jail-breaking one of their members. Though the event had been weeks ago, Jacob still felt his failure deeply.

Jaco stopped in his strolling behind Mr. Bagley. "If I may, Mr. Bart ..."

The other man turned and looked at him quizzically.

"I wanted to apologize again for what happened to your store. My injuries are all just about healed, so I'm happy to help with any reconstruction that still may need to be done."

He smiled. "I appreciate that, Mr. Payne, but we're not in need of any further assistance. Several men of the town have stepped forward to help and we have completed the most elaborate of the repairs."

"I understand. Just let me know if anything comes up." Jacob offered his hand and Mr. Bart shook it.

"Much obliged to you, sir."

Mr. Bagley cleared his throat, calling for Jacob's attention again.

"This way, Mr. Payne," he said, gesturing through the doorway to his office.

Jacob took a deep breath and strode forward. Though he had experienced a brief moment of doubt, wondering if he wanted to curtail his freedom like this, wondering if tying himself to this town even a little bit was what he wanted. But that moment passed. Only a child would think he was being restricted.

Opening a bank account was a simple, small thing that any man would do.

"Can I have Matthew get you coffee?" Mr. Bagley asked, indicating the blond young man waiting anxiously outside the office door.

"Coffee would be welcome," Jacob replied with a smile. "Let's get started."

CHAPTER TWO

Jacob exited the bank in the late morning sunshine. His paperwork with his account details was folded up and safely tucked into the same pocket with his billfold, now unnaturally empty. He patted his pockets, looking for a coin, bill or anything else he might have missed. Although he knew that depositing the bulk of his cash had been the right thing, now in the immediate aftermath, all Jacob could think of was that he needed to get back to work.

He rolled his shoulder, feeling the way his muscles had relaxed. The same shoulder had been dislocated in the skirmish that had destroyed the pharmacy. But now Jacob felt fine. He rolled his shoulder again, reflecting that if he didn't know better he could have forgotten that injury altogether.

He began walking up the boardwalk closer to the center of town, while he decided how else to spend his morning. Tucson was growing. The *Arizona Citizen* was now more than a month old and attracting new subscribers and new residents every day. The stagecoach stop on the way to California made for interesting new characters to pass through town all the time. And, as Jacob had mentioned to Mr. Bagley, his own business *was* booming. For every two good, honest new citizens, there was likely one worthless scamp come to Arizona.

He watched a heavyset man with his hat pulled down low over his face hurrying up the walk on the other side of the street. Jacob had trained himself to notice suspicious activities everywhere, and though he couldn't pin anything on this man other than the fact that he didn't want to be seen, it was enough.

Though generally, Jacob's outlaw tracking had taken him outside the town, with the Slippery Stone Gang showing up in Tucson he could no longer take that for granted. Any man at any time could be an outlaw, or a lead to a criminal that needed to be brought to justice. The bounty hunter hadn't actually pursued a wanted man in a few weeks, but his instincts and inclinations could not be turned off.

The encounter with the Slippery Stone Gang a few weeks previously had put him out of commission. Jacob reminded himself that if pressed he could have actually hit the road, or assisted the U.S. Marshal. He wasn't incapacitated. His injuries were superficial for the most part. Muscles needed to heal and bruises needed to fade, but he had not been completely debilitated.

Instead, Jacob had put himself on voluntary sick leave at the request of one Bonnie Loft. The waitress at the San Xavier Cafe was his friend and—he supposed he was right in calling her this now—his sweetheart. She would never have outright asked Jacob to stop, but he had seen the depth of her concern and wanted to ease her mind.

Besides, he had reminded himself, that's what all his savings had been for, after all. The cash was there so he didn't have to work constantly. When else would he be able to take the time to recuperate than when he could afford to?

Three weeks had seemed like a good length of time to give himself, and Bonnie. Now that he still had several day left, though, Jacob was beginning to regret setting a time limit on himself.

Especially with his billfold now feeling so empty.

Jacob turned his feet and headed north to the U.S. Marshal's office.

The three weeks was almost up. Close enough, he told himself. Skipping a couple days wouldn't hurt, and he could look and see what needed doing.

When he reached the jail, Jacob knocked lightly and let himself in. After the jailbreak, in the weeks since Jacob had been active, the door had been replaced and reinforced. Even still, Jacob would be surprised to have found it locked. The front window let enough light in to illuminate the marshal's desk and the shelves behind it. The tall, pole-thin man was hunched over the desk, writing furiously. Owen Santos was one of the few men in all of the Arizona Territory to be taller than Jacob; as such he always looked cramped leaning over the desk in his office. This was a man who, like Jacob, did far better out of doors, without his long legs folded underneath a desk.

"Jacob Payne," he said, brightening up when he noticed his visitor. "I was beginning to think I'd never see you again. Figured you might've taken up knitting or some other quiet, indoor hobby."

"Yes, yes, very funny," Jacob said with a grin. "I know. It feels like it has been forever since I've been on a case."

"How long has it been, actually?" Santos said. "So much has happened, I barely know what day it is."

"Just under three weeks since the jailbreak. Eighteen days."

"Eighteen days," Santos repeated. "Not as though you're counting or anything."

Jacob chuckled. "Eighteen days feels like more than enough. I came to see what you've got for me, Marshal. Blaze is chomping at the bit to get out on the road again."

"Blaze is, huh? Yeah, I let my horse make the decisions, too," Santos said. "Glad to see you're feeling better, Payne. Truly."

"Well, you know that I would have been happy to be of service any time, right?"

"I do know. Thank you." He leaned back in his chair. "But I also know that a certain waitress friend of ours would have died of anxiety if I had asked such a thing of you. She's the one that keeps me in apple pie, and I'm happy to keep her happy."

"Smart man," Jacob said. "Just show me

where you're keeping the wanted posters and I'll see what I can do."

"Oh, yes," Santos said, distractedly digging through the piles of paperwork on his desk. "Somewhere around here. Give me a moment."

Jacob hid his surprise. He had expected Santos to jump at the opportunity to hand over his worst jobs to the bounty hunter. It wasn't vanity to remember that the marshal himself had called Jacob the best bounty hunter in five territories. With the way crime was spreading to the frontier, he had expected a stack of paper as tall as he was.

Instead, the marshal was actually having to search for the material.

"You must have been busy," Jacob ventured, "to have so few jobs for me."

"Me?" Santos looked up at Jacob in surprise. It appeared to be taking him a moment to register what he had said. "Oh, well ... A bit, I guess. You know how dumb some men can be. Me and the deputies got a half-dozen stage-coach robbers in one go, all camping just outside town. Didn't even set up a guard for their camp or nothing. But, no, not me. There may have been fewer jobs, I suppose, but for the most part this has all been the work of a new man in town."

"Oh?" Again, Jacob was grateful for his poker face. He successfully hid his surprise and, yes, a little dismay at hearing the marshal's words.

Santos had stood now, digging through a different stack of paperwork on the corner of the desk closest to Jacob.

"Name's, uh, Clifford Pierce. I think he said he's from Illinois maybe. Or Iowa? Indiana? I can't remember. Somewhere north of here, for certain. He won't stop griping about the heat at least. Claims this is unnatural for November. But the man does good work, so I can't fault him an opinion about the weather."

"Clifford Pierce."

"It was right fortunate he showed up here when he did. I think he might have moved on pretty quickly—the heat, like I say—if I hadn't been so pressing. With you out of commission the jobs were just piling up and it seemed as though we'd never get out from under it. I thought maybe word would spread that there was no law at all in Arizona."

"But, Marshal, forgive me," Jacob began hesitatingly. "I wasn't out of commission. You could have called on me at any time. You did, in fact, before Olmos, didn't you? If you needed help so badly, why didn't you ask me?"

Jacob's voice was calm and even, but he could feel a stream of adrenaline surging through him. Who was this Clifford Pierce that the marshal was so praising? Jacob reminded himself that Arizona did not belong to him, and the more men committed to upholding the law the better.

"Oh, I know, Payne," Santos said dismissively. "I just didn't want— Aha!"

The marshal seized up a handful of papers from under the large stone that sat on the shelf behind his desk. Jacob had been meaning to ask him about that stone, but now was not the time.

"You find what you're looking for?"

"Yep." Santos beamed triumphantly. "Here you are, Payne. All the criminals who are about to meet their match."

He handed over the stack of wanted posters to the bounty hunter who thumbed through them quickly. Where normally Jacob had his pick of several dozen jobs of varying degrees of difficulty, now he had only fourteen or fifteen. After a quick perusal, Jacob surmised that this Clifford Pierce fellow had scooped up all but the most difficult bounties in the territory. And Jacob wasn't fool enough to think that he had done that deliberately. If Elliott "Slippery"

Stone was still worth several thousand dollars, there was no doubt that Pierce was at least trying to find his trail.

Jacob Payne was confident in his skills. He knew that given enough time any one of these dastardly men could find their way to his capture. But time was not something he wanted to spend right now.

Who was this Clifford Pierce?

"Oh, hey. One more," Santos said, handing Jacob another wanted poster. "This one came just this morning. But, you know, Jacob. If you're not feeling right—"

"I'm fine." He offered Santos a tight smile. "Thanks. I'm good. I'm all right. Looking forward to getting back on the trail, as a matter of fact."

He skimmed over the outlaw's details that the marshal had just handed him. Stagecoach robber. Five-foot-nine with black hair and beard. Bounty of only forty dollars. Ross Kendall. Last seen in Valencia.

"Can you tell me any more about this one?" he asked, indicating.

"Let me see." Santos took it back from him and skimmed. "Valencia, huh? I think Pierce was headed that way last I talked to him. Much more dangerous man he was after though. If I remember right, the sheriff who took down the details of this Kendall man's case told me he had somewhat botched the robbery. Only got off with a couple billfolds and apparently left behind a whole chest full of luxury items headed for a hotel. Maybe he's too lazy to want to have to sell anything." Santos chuckled.

"So, not the sharpest tool in the shed, I take it. Did you say Pierce went to Valencia? Think he's still there?"

"Could be. Depends I suppose. Haven't heard from him in a couple days, though."

Jacob nodded to himself and considered the ramifications of this job. Taking him that far away from home, for only forty dollars. But, then again, maybe whoever Pierce was after would make it worthwhile. Jacob felt an urge to see this man for himself, but pushed it down.

"You can count on me, Marshal," he said. "And if your friend Mr. Pierce comes in again, I'd like to meet him."

Santos frowned. "Meet him? All right, Payne. I'll tell him. Good luck."

Jacob tipped his hat and left the office without another word.

CHAPTER THREE

As Jacob made his way from the marshal's office, he digested all this new information and what his next steps needed to be. Valencia was a far enough trek that he'd have to at least purchase more supplies for the road. Blaze was well rested, but Jacob would have a few stops to make.

And figure out how to break the news to Bonnie that he was ending his convalescence early. And leaving town.

His feet had carried him while his mind was on other matters, and soon Jacob realized he was on the same road as the San Xavier Cafe and the Golden Saddle Saloon. He looked at his pocket watch—it was right about lunchtime.

The perfect time to grab a bite and start laying the groundwork for leaving town.

Both establishments were right near each other. Jacob made a split-second decision. It caused him a brief pang of guilt, but he assured himself that the last thing Bonnie needed while she was trying to wait on other patrons was to be worrying about him. Jacob would instead go the Golden Saddle and see what he could learn about Clifford Pierce.

Besides, he told himself. Men there were far more likely to have news of Ross Kendall, if there was any to be had.

Jacob turned left and made his way to the saloon, pushing down his feelings of guilt for disappointing Bonnie.

As he made his way inside, Jacob waved to Lucky and Abe, the gamblers who spent most of their days playing—working—from the table in the corner of the saloon. They had been accused of cheating in the past but, from what Jacob knew, a thorough investigation had concluded that these two men were just excellent gamblers.

So good, in fact, that their reputation had spread throughout the Arizona Territory and nearby. Men from California, Utah, Texas and farther were making pilgrimages to Tucson just to try their luck against the pair. Abe had been vocally proud of the fact, and Jacob could just laugh. All this hubbub had done for him was confirm he shouldn't be playing against these two. Now or ever.

And yet, when he walked in, Abe tried to wave him over. Jacob shook his head and made his way to the bar instead.

As he sat and got the bartender's attention, it struck him that for however long that Pierce had been in Tucson, not a single one of Jacob's friends in town had mentioned the man to him. Surely at least one of them must have met him. Even if Pierce was rarely there in between hunting for outlaws, he would have to come back sometime. And both he and his horse would have to eat. But for some reason, Jacob had been kept in the dark.

"What'll you have?" the man asked.

Jacob had previously met Pete Pendleton, but had not yet had occasion to have any length of conversation with him. He did, after all, spend most of his time at the San Xavier Cafe instead of here in the saloon. But from what Jacob knew of Pete, he'd be helpful if he could be. He liked to talk, that was certain.

The bounty hunter ordered a beer and a serving of whatever was in the kitchen that day. He fell into musing as he waited for his dinner.

The more he thought about it, the more it occurred to him that it was strange that he hadn't heard about Pierce before that morning. Were the other men in Tucson hiding something from him?

Pete came back with Jacob's food, setting it down in front of him clumsily. The plate tipped so far some of the gravy spilled off onto the bar.

"Whoops," Pete said, with no real regret in his tone. "Now let me get you that beer."

"Thanks. I wonder if you might help me out with something. You heard of a man called Clifford Pierce?" Jacob asked, trying to sound casual.

"Pierce?" Pete furrowed his brow, thinking as he poured. "Oh, yeah. Pierce. He's been in here a few times. He's kept a room upstairs for a couple weeks, though I don't think he actually sleeps here all that much. He's a bounty hunter, ain't he?"

"That's what they tell me." Jacob took a bite of potatoes, dripping with gravy.

"Yeah, Pierce is an interesting fella, all right," Pete continued. A couple older men at the far end of the bar were trying to get his attention, but the bartender was either too distracted or too indifferent to go do his job. "Seems awfully proud of himself, that man. That or he's a flannel-mouthed liar." Pete chuckled.

"*Sir!*"

The bearded man on the end finally gave up trying to be polite and yelled at Pete. The bartender hustled over to help. Alone with his thoughts, Jacob went over his mental list of all the preparations he needed to make to go after Ross Kendall. The forty dollars he was to make would get eaten up pretty quick, but Jacob knew he needed to get back in the saddle.

A few moments later, Pete was back in front of Jacob, ready to gossip and jaw all afternoon if need be. Jacob wondered if the saloon was so empty because of Pete's chattiness or the quality of the food or both.

"I heard you broke your ribs or some such, Payne. Is that true?"

Jacob scoffed. "No. Not true. Where'd you hear that?"

"I dunno." He shrugged. "Who knows where I hear anything, with all the comings and goings in this place. But you been around a lot, haven't you? In town?"

"Yep. I did suffer some injuries a couple weeks ago. And my girl was worried about me, so to ease her mind I've been staying put. But now I'm all healed up and ready to hit the road. I'll likely be heading west to Valencia in the morning."

"Valencia? Funny coincidence you're going there. Last I heard from Pierce, he was following a lead up to Valencia too."

"Was he?" Jacob prompted, pleased to have led Pete right to the topic. "Any idea what his plans were?"

"Like I say, he might be a big talker. But the way I heard it Pierce had a connection to a member of the Slippery Stone Gang and he was going to go after Stone himself."

Jacob was both taken aback and unsurprised. From the little he knew about Pierce, it would have been out of character for him to not go after the biggest fish. The detail that he had a connection and a lead in Valencia was news to Jacob, though. Was it luck or Providence that Jacob was planning on heading to the same place?

In a flash, Jacob pictured the icy blue eyes and brown curly hair of Elliott Stone. If any bounty was going to capture this renegade, it had to be Jacob Payne. He would become a legend in the territory. Hell, in the whole country.

He couldn't let Clifford Pierce get there first.

"Anything else you can tell me about Pierce?" Jacob shoveled more food into his mouth to keep himself quiet. The longer he let Pete talk unhindered, the more he would reveal.

"Well, I dunno." Pete dug a finger into one ear, squinting one eye at the pain as he pushed it deeper. "He's the kinda man that talks about himself a lot. Though, now that I think about it, I'm not sure he's really *said* all that much, if you get my meaning. There's a lot around here that seemed charmed enough by him, though."

Jacob nodded. He did know. U.S. Marshal Santos seemed downright smitten with the other bounty hunter, in fact.

"And, like I say, he talked a lot about bringing in Elliott Stone. Only God knows if that will come to pass." Pete shrugged again.

"The marshal led me to believe that Pierce has brought in a lot of outlaws in the last couple weeks."

"Maybe. I dunno."

Jacob and the bartender regarded each other for another moment as the former continued to eat. He wasn't sure what to think, but one thing was clear. Jacob would need to go to Valencia. He would capture Ross Kendall if nothing else.

He would again be available for all the difficult and dangerous jobs in the territory.

Jacob had taken a long enough break and now it was time for action.

He'd have to break the news to Bonnie before he left, though.

CHAPTER FOUR

Jacob had a few options. He wanted to get on the road soon, but he didn't want to worry or alarm Bonnie before he left town. Instead of visiting her at the cafe, after he ate and chatted with Pete, he waited on the porch of her boarding house for her to get home. Bonnie's landlady, Mrs. Withers, threatened to throw him off her property, but ultimately decided that the bounty hunter had too many official connections in Tucson for her to risk overtly offending him.

Instead, she ignored him.

Jacob sat on the porch, in the afternoon heat, without offer of any refreshment for more than an hour. But he didn't want to miss a single moment of Bonnie's time, as long as he was still in town. So he waited as long as was necessary.

When she turned to walk up the front path of the home, her whole face lit up in recognizing him.

"Why! Jacob Payne. What are you doing here?" Her question felt loaded with concern. While she may have gotten used to his changing plans and putting himself in danger on a regular basis, that didn't make it ever any easier to hear.

"I need to talk to you, please." He stood and took her hand. "Do you want to change or eat first or—"

"No, no." She waved a hand dismissing his concerns. "Come sit. Tell me everything."

Jacob took a deep breath, said a silent prayer of gratitude for this patient woman, and launched into his news. He felt like so many conversations with her recently had been the same—he had to go to work. He had to leave Tucson. But somehow this time felt different, although he couldn't have put his finger on why.

"All right," she said, when he finished. "You're leaving tomorrow? Is there anything I can do to help?"

"You darling girl," he said, almost in a whisper. Jacob caught up her hand and kissed it. "Thank you for understanding."

"Well, you know, Jacob. Just because I understand doesn't mean I like it," she teased. "You told me just yesterday that your ribs we're still all bruised up."

"You're right. Of course. You're right. But I'll never forgive myself if I let myself get further behind. This is just something I have to do. For me."

"Further behind what?" she asked, frowning. "Are you— You're not worried about money, are you?"

"No." Jacob silently cursed his slip of the tongue. He backtracked. "Maybe that's not the right word. Behind the outlaw, so to speak. If he was last seen in Valencia, Lord knows where he could be now."

She seemed satisfied by his answer and didn't ask any more questions. Instead, she leaned over from her seat and rested her head on his shoulder.

"I'll miss you, Jacob," she said quietly. "Come home to me soon, please."

"I will. I promise. As soon as I can."

He held her in an embrace, trying to sear the memory into his brain, as it would be all of her he had to hold on to for the next several days.

. . .

The road to Valencia was longer than he expected. Even keeping on the road constantly, with short breaks for food and water, Jacob planned to be riding Blaze for nearly two full days. The days were growing shorter now as November wore on, and Jacob could only count on ten or eleven hours of light.

He knew what he was signing up for. Two days of travel—four total when he went home—not including the time it took him to track down and capture Ross Kendall, and all for only forty dollars. He could afford it. Forty dollars was not nothing, but it was also far less than he had commanded for a bounty in quite a while.

Jacob tried to put that all out of his mind. A bounty hunter's job was to get the man, not to wait around for something more lucrative to come along. But as he and Blaze walked the mile after mile to Valencia, he turned over the situation in his mind.

Maybe the reason bounty hunters seemed to have such a poor reputation was because they all would have turned down this job. So many of the men who went into this line of work were just aiming to earn money for shooting other men. Maybe he was being foolish. Or maybe he was just the only bounty hunter in the territory with any innate sense of justice.

Jacob whistled to himself as Blaze plodded, step after step westward to Valencia. From what Jacob had been told, it was a small town, just begun and on the cusp of booming. A small gold lode had been discovered in the hills and word was beginning to spread. As it was a mining town, Jacob knew he could expect even more lawlessness and less gentility than usual.

No wonder Ross Kendall had gone there.

For two full days, Jacob rode in silence, alone under the November sun with nothing to do but think. Fortunately, Blaze wasn't much of a conversationalist either, and Jacob soon filled his mind with ideas and dreams for the future. With the cash he had deposited in the bank, he could now begin planning for the possibility of staying in the west. As such, he had a number of things that needed to be decided.

None of which were pressing, but all of which filled the time on his long trek to Valencia.

At the end of the second day, Jacob saw a sprinkling of lights along the horizon at the foot of the hills. The sun was just setting as he rode the final miles into the brand new mining town.

Even though it was after dark, the town was still bustling. Jacob heard the unmistakable sounds of hammers being driven into nails, saws cutting through wood and barrels being heaved. Men cursing and yelling instructions. Woven through all of it the lilting laughter of women trying to tempt new customers. He reined his horse at the top of what appeared to be the main street of Valencia and took it all in.

CHAPTER FIVE

In spite of the busy, noisy streets of Valencia, Jacob felt wary. A mining boom town would be the destination of the worst of the worst, the men with no morals and no qualms about breaking the law.

Jacob sniffed the air. He had always had a stronger sense of smell than most people, and in this line of work it had helped him more often than not. As he walked Blaze slowly down the main street of Valencia, Jacob didn't detect anything out of the ordinary. Not yet at least.

He smelled food cooking, horses, unwashed men, campfires and gunpowder. Jacob smelled fresh cut lumber and—he sniffed again—what he might be able to identify as a mountain spring. There was a metallic

tang to water that came down from the mountains in Arizona that he was just learning to
recognize.

Jacob nudged Blaze forward down the
street.

If one could call it a street.

It was a flat, dirt stretch of ground, deeply
rutted in places, manure piled practically everywhere. Several wagons passed by Jacob going
the opposite direction. There was no real indi-
cation where one should walk as opposed to
where the campsites could start. It was chaotic.

From where he sat atop the horse, as far as
Jacob could see there only appeared to be one
building with a roof, and even that was still only
half built. The church. There was at least one
man of God in this pandemonium and he had
been the first to put down roots.

Jacob looked around at the rest of the citizens of Valencia as he continued down the path.
This town was growing, that much was clear.
Some of the citizens appeared to be building—
homes, places of business, hitching posts. But
many of them seemed to be content in their
tents, cooking game over fires outside not six
feet from where their neighbors were setting up
their own tents or boiling their own water.
Behind the first row of campsites, more men

were setting up their own accommodations farther from the center of town.

As Jacob continued to lead Blaze down the street, some of the citizens tipped their hats and greeted him, but for the most part he was ignored. Few had time for a second glance at yet another new face. These men were likely used to newcomers showing up all the time. Realizing that Valencia was little more than a tent city, Jacob tried to decide where to go first. It was after supper. He needed to get his horse settled for the night. But with the exception of the half-built church, he couldn't see anywhere to go.

Maybe the pastor would have a suggestion for him.

Jacob dismounted and walked to the church on foot, where he found an older man sitting in the open doorway. He looked to be old enough to be Jacob's father, and sat fanning himself with a bowler hat. Though the evening was cool, the older man's shirt was soaked through with sweat. All around him sat the evidence of a day of manual labor: a hammer, tin cup full of loose nails, a damp handkerchief and the beginnings of studs for a wall.

This was no delicate flower as Jacob had known some men back east. Those fellows had convinced themselves that God would take care of them simply by virtue of their blessed existence. No, this man of cloth, this older gentleman who seemed to have discovered a second life on the western frontier, evidently lived by the adage 'God helps those who help themselves.'

And as such, he seemed like the most ideal person for Jacob to turn to for assistance.

"Evening, sir," Jacob said as he removed his hat. "I wonder if you might be able to help me."

The older man lit up when he saw him, stood to greet Jacob, and shook his hand vigorously.

"Happy to, young man. Happy to. My name is Pastor McGorry. God calls us to champion the cause of the stranger, so if there's anything I can do for you I certainly will. You're new to Valencia, aren't ya? Care to sit?"

Jacob looped Blaze's reins around one of the studs of the wall of the church. Not ideal, but he trusted his horse. He sat on the steps of the church next to the pastor.

"Much obliged, sir. My name is Jacob Payne."

"What brings you to town, Mr. Payne?"

"I'm a bounty hunter."

"Ah." The pastor laughed. "So you and I

share the same business, you might say. Seeking the souls of men who have strayed from the path."

"Something like that." Jacob grinned. "I'm wondering if you can give me some tips. I'm in town for ... oh, I don't know. A couple days maybe. Is there anywhere around here I can board my horse and myself?"

Pastor McGorry put a hand on either side of his face and rubbed his cheeks hard. He looked like he hadn't shaved in a few days; his cheeks must have felt like sandpaper. White and silver stubble peppered his face. Jacob had to stop himself from wincing when it seemed as though the man was bent on poking himself in the eye as he rubbed vigorously.

"Well now, let me see. It's true we don't yet have a hotel set up for visitors. Not sure we've even had any yet. 'Sfar as I can tell all these men aim to live here themselves. I'm sure we can find an empty bed for you somewhere, friend. But a livery! That we have in spades. Or, well, two of them, at least. A pair of liveries." He grinned at Jacob. "Come. I'll show you."

Jacob allowed his horse and himself to be led.

Following a local was one of his favorite tricks when arriving in a new town. Some men thought asking for help was a detriment, but Jacob had only ever seen the benefit. When all he had to do was keep track of the back of the man in front of him, it cleared up his space and observation to take in more details around him. Sometimes that just meant entertainment. But more often than not he was able to pick up clues and hints that he could use for the rest of his work.

And as they walked to the far end of Valencia, Jacob noticed several things.

Firstly, though he had been correct in his initial estimation that the church was the only building in town with even a partial roof, a closer examination revealed that that would not long be the case. All along the main road, Jacob spied the foundations and beginnings of more permanent buildings. Floorboards were being installed. Walls were going up. It might still be a few months yet before this place felt anything like settled, but it was on its way.

Second, in spite of the lack of permanent structure to house the establishment, there was one place of business that seemed far and away the busiest. It was no surprise to Jacob to hear the lively noises coming out of a large tent in the middle of town. No matter where they were, no matter how hard they worked, men would always need some refreshment. Both of the liquid and feminine varieties. It was a smart man who was the first to offer such sustenance in a new town like Valencia. Of course the saloon was a rollicking place, even with canvas walls.

He slowed his walk as much as he could without losing Pastor McGorry. Jacob peered into the tent; if Ross Kendall was in Valencia, it was likely as not he was in the saloon. A rough, handpainted sign reading "The Watering Hole" hung above the opening to the tent. Unfortunately, it was so crowded inside that Jacob was unable to make out many faces, let alone identify the one he was looking for.

He would have to return to the Watering Hole for a more thorough search.

And most importantly, Jacob noticed that though Valencia may be on its way to becoming a town, it wasn't yet. This was in no way a community. There wasn't one thing, or even two, to which he could point to confirm this. It was merely a feeling, a sense Jacob had, that each person he passed was out for himself only.

Few greeted him; many considered him suspiciously as he passed. Men sat alone, hunched over their meal made for one. Others passed Jacob going in the opposite direction and didn't even meet his eye.

That was a dangerous situation to be in when he was hunting for outlaws. If Jacob couldn't count on the good nature and integrity of the men around him, his position was much more dire. He had many a time found himself on his own against the worst men in the territory, and knowing that this could be the same situation was useful.

All this he saw in the six minutes it took Pastor McGorry to find the livery. Or, one of the liveries. Jacob didn't ask why he chose this one over the other, but when the man running it offered to brush Blaze down and take care of him right away, the bounty hunter didn't hesitate. If he was vetted by the pastor, this place of business would be good enough for him.

"Now that's for your horse," McGorry said, again holding his face in his hands. "Now for yourself. I'm sorry, young man. I'd offer you a cot myself if I had one to spare. But I'm all out of extras to give away. I spend my own nights on the floor of my yet-to-be-completed church."

"Don't worry about me, Pastor," Jacob said, holding up his hand to forestall any further protestations. "If I can't find a cot, the ground will do for me as well. That's how I spent last night after all."

"Oh, yes, well, I suppose that's true." He chuckled. "Nevertheless, I think there might be something we can do for you. Let's go see the Beasley brothers."

CHAPTER SIX

Pastor McGorry led the way back up the main street of Valencia, stopping not far from where his half-built church sat. It was another canvas tent, much smaller than the one housing the Watering Hole, but still tall enough for a man to stand upright within.

"Wes?" Pastor McGorry called as they walked up to the doorway.

Above the opening in the tent was another handwritten sign: Beasley Bros. Hardware. Simple, to the point. As they got closer, Jacob could see that the tent itself was full of goods. Rope, saws, barrels of nails, boots, hats, pans, pickaxes, lanterns and on and on. Several tables and ramshackle shelves cobbled together that held any number of supplies a man would need in a frontier town like this. The interior of the tent was only about twelve by twelve feet, but was holding enough wares to supply the entire town.

These Beasley brothers must be smart, getting in early to sell picks and shovels to the miners. They'd make a mint, thought Jacob. And might be the only folks in all of Valencia who would have an extra cot for him.

"Raymond? Wes?" the pastor called again.

"Here! Here, Pastor," a harried-looking man gasped out as he poked his head through a break in the back of the tent. He smoothed down the front of his coat. "I'm so sorry. I only stepped out for a moment— Hey there, friend."

This last was directed at Jacob. The bounty hunter noted the change in tone from the other man. From casual friendliness with the pastor, he had switched over to charmingly polished for his potential customer.

"Good evening," Jacob said, shaking the hand that was offered.

"This here's Wes Beasley. Wes, this is Mr. Payne. He's only in town a short while and we wondered if you might have an extra cot to offer him."

"A bed? Just for a few nights?"

"Maybe less. Depends on how quickly I can find this outlaw I'm after."

Jacob could see the thoughts tumbling in the man's head, calculations over what a bed might be worth to the visitor to Valencia. The bounty hunter smiled, slightly, waiting the brief moment while the store owner battled with himself. Greed and capitalism or hospitality and generosity. As with any other man in the west, this decision could go either way.

"If not, it's no matter, Mr. Beasley. I've slept on the ground out-of-doors more nights than I can count. It'll be dry tonight and that's good enough for me."

That decided it.

"Nonsense," he said. "My brother and I are happy to support the work of a lawman, even if he is a bounty hunter."

Jacob smiled, uncertainly. "Thank you."

"Here's what I'll do for you. We got room in our sleeping tent back yonder. I'll get a cot set up for you there for as long as you need it. Inside and everything." He raised his eyebrows, sure he was impressing the other man. "I'm sure you know, desert nights get cold around these parts. I've got an extra quilt too. I'll feed you three square meals a day as long as you're here and I can even throw in a hot bath once every three days. All for only five dollars a day. Can't do any better than that around here, I assure you."

"Mighty kind of you, though I'm not sure I will need all that." Privately Jacob wondered if anyone else had been fool enough to pay such prices. "This the first time you've offered such a deal to a visitor to Valencia?"

"It is." He laughed. "Well, first time I got as far as making an offer that is. Just a couple days ago there was another man come through here. Seemed to think that he wouldn't be in town long enough to even need a bed, though now that I think about it I'm pretty sure he's still here."

"Oh, that's right," said Pastor McGorry, lighting up. "Talkative fellow. I believe he was a bounty hunter as well, now's I think about it."

That got Jacob's attention. "A bounty hunter? Don't suppose you can recall this man's name, can you?"

Pastor McGorry screwed up his face in concentration, rubbing his cheeks hard as he thought. "No ... No, I think it's gone from my mind. It's like a sieve up here some days. Seems the only thing that sticks is the Holy Bible. Even my children's names aren't always ready on my tongue." He laughed. "But, like Wes says, he might still be in Valencia. We can find him and introduce you, I'm sure."

"I'm sure," Jacob said.

"What do you say, Mr. Payne? Will you let the Beasley brothers host you while you're here?"

"You don't need to talk to the other brother first?" he queried. "I don't want to be taking advantage of someone's home without his say."

"Nope. Not a bit of it," Wes scoffed. "Raymond's the one hankering after more lawmen around here. Seems to think he'll get to be the first sheriff of Valencia just by virtue of sheer will. I'm sure he's out campaigning now. Buying fellows all the drinks he can."

"He'd make a wonderful sheriff," Pastor McGorry interjected.

"Maybe," he said with a shrug. "But that'd leave him less time for the store. I can't do this all myself." Wes looked irritated. Wherever his brother was at that moment, Jacob felt sure that Wes would have rather he be in that tent with them. "But, as I say ... he's a fan of the more law-abiding citizens and would be happy to encourage a man like you to stick around. Especially if you take an outlaw or two with you when you go."

"That bad around here?" Jacob asked.

Wes nodded with a deep sigh. "Can't expect much else in a town that didn't even exist a few months ago. Once word got around that gold was discovered, Valencia became a siren call for all the lazy and unscrupulous men in the area. All the men who came west to seek their fortunes but then somehow pissed it all away in a dancehall? Those are the men that show up first in a town like this. In a few months we'll have more men from the east, including the big shots who buy the claims out from under more desperate men. But right now, it's precarious. Precarious, I tell you."

That sounded exactly like the kind of place Jacob needed to be. He'd keep an eye out for Ross Kendall and his forty-dollar bounty, but there was likely a greater good he could render. If Clifford Pierce had come here after Slippery Stone, it seemed a good bet. Maybe Jacob himself could find Stone first. He had, after all, had far more interaction with the man and others of his gang than this fly-by-night from Iowa or Indiana or wherever he hailed from.

Yes, this all sounded just about right. Exactly where Jacob needed to be after his weeks away from the hunt.

"Well, then, Mr. Beasley, if you feel certain

your brother won't mind, I'll take you up on the offer, if you can come down a bit on the price."

Wes looked surprised for a split second, but the shock was gone in an instant and he merely grinned pleasantly. The two bartered for a quick minute before both could be pleased with the deal.

"Wonderful. That's wonderful, Payne. I'm proud to host you. Mighty proud. And anything else I can help you with while you're here, just don't hesitate to ask."

"You boys have supper yet?" Pastor McGorry asked. "I was just thinking about rustling up something when Mr. Payne here came up."

"I could do with some supper," Jacob said. "I'm happy to contribute whatever necessary. I believe I've got a small bag penny of candy in my saddlebag somewhere."

"Well doesn't that just beat all?" Pastor McGorry said. "I have got quite the sweet tooth, my boy. It's been an age since I've had a candy."

"I'm sure the Bible probably has a verse about sharing blessings with others, doesn't it?" Jacob said with a grin. "I'd be much obliged if you would help me eat it all."

"And what about you, Mr. Beasley?"

"It's tempting, I must say. But I can't leave the store unguarded."

Before Jacob could offer a suggestion, their conversation was interrupted by the sound of gunshots. All three men rushed out into the street to see what was happening.

CHAPTER SEVEN

Jacob, Pastor McGorry and Wes Beasley stood in the dirt road just in front of the Beasley Brothers Hardware store and looked frantically around for the source of the gunshots. Other men were abandoning their own tents, projects, and cook fires to do the same. Though the population of Valencia was still only barely in the three digits, it seemed as though every one of them was in the street at this moment.

And every one of them were focusing their attention on the same thing—the fighting just outside the Watering Hole.

It was clear there were two men going at it. Another shot fired, and Jacob could see the gunmen held the pistol above his head, shooting into the air. Whatever this fight was about, it wasn't deadly. Not yet.

The bounty hunter tried to push his way through the crowd, but everyone he tried to pass ignored him. One man, a full head shorter than Jacob, literally growled at him as he tried to make his way through.

The yelling grew louder, as did the crowd, egging on the two combatants, placing bets and taking sides.

Since Jacob was just over six feet tall, he eventually was able to edge past enough onlookers to be able to see over the heads of those remaining. There was a small circle of men around the pair of fighters. One of the two adversaries was well passed drunk, on his way to blacking out. The other was inebriated, but clearly more in possession of his faculties. The first was short with black hair and full black beard, the second had a mop of curly brown hair on his uncovered head.

Jacob stared hard at the two men. From this distance, in the evening light there was plenty of opportunity for him to be wrong. But the more he looked, the more he watched, the more certain he was.

The falling-over-drunk man, the man in the black duster, was none other than Ross Kendall.

For a man allegedly on the run from the law, he sure was drawing plenty of attention to himself, not only in his dropping his guard and becoming so intoxicated, but also in picking a fight and taking it to the street.

He was a fool. A fool who was going to be brought to justice.

Jacob tried again to push his way through the crowd to the men fighting. He would take charge of the situation, talk down the curly-headed man and place Kendall in custody. Just forming this plan in his mind, Jacob relaxed a little. It wasn't often that capturing an outlaw became this easy, and he was grateful.

More determined than he had been before, Jacob began pushing through the crowd to the men at the center. More than once a big drunk challenged his forward progress. More than once, Jacob had to ignore, threaten or in one case, elbow a man out of his way.

"Mr. Payne! Mr. Payne," a voice called from behind him.

Confused and distracted, Jacob turned around to see Pastor McGorry pushing through the crowd in his wake.

"Mr. Payne, son, you don't want to get mixed up in this."

No, thought Jacob. I don't want to have to explain myself to you.

But to the sweet old man, he only said, "I have to."

"No, you don't. The good book teaches us to help those in need, but I think we can safely say that doesn't apply to barroom brawls," he said with a twinkle in his eye. "You're new to town, so maybe you ain't been around disagreements like this. It's best to just let it run its course."

"I've been around plenty of fights, Pastor McGorry—" he began.

"Not like this. No, sir. I tell you, I made the mistake of trying to break up a fight when I first got to town. I remembered Psalm eighty-two four, you see, and thought it was my duty to protect these men from themselves. It was a night just like this..."

Jacob sighed. He had to lean closer to hear the old man's reminiscences over the noise of the crowd. He peeked back over his shoulder, relieved to see that his quarry was still in the same place. Jacob turned back to the pastor, intending to extricate himself from this impromptu sermon as soon as he could without giving offense.

"Yes, sir, a night just like this when I was tired from the day's labor and the other men were still pouring into town. On that night, however, the fight stayed within the tent. I heard the yelling from my church, right as I was finishing my supper and thinking about heading to bed for the night."

"I understand, Pastor, but you know my situation is different. This is my job—"

"It's my job too, young man," the pastor said, shaking a finger scoldingly in the big man's face. "It's my job to protect my flock, even if these boys in particular might not have considered themselves part of the flock as yet. Anyway, as I say, I heard the ruckus and made my way to the Watering Hole. The crowd parted for me, bless their hearts. Everyone has just been so kind to me since I got here, and that night not a single soul got in my way.

"Yes, sir," he closed his eyes as he remembered the scene, "the crowd parted like the Red Sea and I walked into the fracas as bold as a cock in a henhouse. I didn't even get half a sentence out of my mouth before I got bowled over by one of the sinners therein. Now, I'm not saying the man meant to hit me, but I did put myself in the middle of it after all.

"Not only did I not stop the fight and not stop those men from hurting each other, but I walked away with two black eyes, a bruised rib and a swollen wrist. Lucky I didn't break anything, to be honest, but I think some other good Samaritan dragged me out of the circle before more damage could be done. So you see, son, barroom fights are the devil's work and the Lord Almighty certainly don't expect us to take on the devil armed with nothing but our two fists."

"Forgive me, Pastor, but you've not changed my mind." The older man seemed about to interrupt, so Jacob raised his voice and carried on. "I've been entrusted to carry out the law, which includes taking that man"—he gestured over his shoulder—"back to Tucson with me. You're right that I might get hurt in the process, but this is still something I have to do."

When he finally convinced the pastor that he was going through this with or without his support, Jacob turned back to the fight. He caught the eye of one of the men standing nearby who smirked at him. Jacob didn't know how many had heard his conversation with the pastor, but he knew that this fight was about to get a lot more interesting for everyone involved.

When he turned back to the brawl, Jacob saw immediately that Ross Kendall was losing. There were now two additional men in the circle with them, ostensibly holding Kendall in place so the other man could get in his blows, but it was clear to everyone watching that they were also serving to hold the passed out man upright.

If this had ever been a fair fight it certainly was not now.

The curly haired man had discarded his pistol in the dirt at his feet and was laying into the outlaw with both hands. A fist to the ribs, to the gut, to the face, to the temple. Kendall was getting the worst of it with no attempt to defend himself. Jacob could have almost felt sorry for the man—he seemed such an incompetent kind of outlaw.

But whether he deserved the beating or not was not the question.

Jacob stepped forward into the circle.

"Stop!" he yelled in a commanding tone.

The curly haired man was surprised into halting his punches and turned to see who dared get between his victim and him.

"You two," Jacob said, gesturing at the helpers. "Let him go."

They seemed reluctant to comply, until Jacob took the next few steps toward them. They both dropped Kendall's arms, though at different times so the man hung awkwardly by one arm for a moment, before collapsing into the dirt.

The two helpers looked warily at Jacob, then at the other man, the curly haired man who seemed to be in charge.

But Jacob ignored the opponent. While he may have been dishonorable to be fighting an unconscious Kendall, that wasn't against the law and Jacob didn't want to tussle with him if he didn't have to.

The bounty hunter reached down to seize Ross Kendall, lifting him bodily off the ground and setting him on his feet. With one hand firmly around his upper arm, Jacob held him in place, slapping his cheek gently to wake him up.

"You, Ross Kendall, are under arrest." To the curly haired man Jacob said, "I'm sorry to have to interrupt, sir, but this man is coming with me."

Jacob felt a flash of familiarity when the man turned his ice blue eyes on him.

"Like hell he is," the man said darkly.

CHAPTER EIGHT

"This man is going nowhere with you," the curly haired man said, pointing his pistol at Jacob.

The bounty hunter paused and frowned. His hand still held a vise-like grip on Ross Kendall's upper arm, and it seemed a matter of only seconds before Jacob became the only thing holding him upright. Bringing the outlaw to consciousness was a temporary fix. It was understandable that this opponent might want to finish his own fight with the outlaw, but Jacob wasn't about to let go.

"Seems we're going to have to disagree about that, sir," Jacob said calmly. "Sorry about that. This man is wanted by the U.S. Marshal in Tucson and I have been charged with bringing him in. You don't want to stand between him and the law, now, do you?"

The other man laughed, softly at first but then it grew into a disrespectful guffaw that surprised Jacob.

"The law? Well, boy, you must not know who you're talking to if you think you can threaten *me* with the law."

Jacob smarted under the insult of being called boy. He would eat his shoe if this man was older than he was. He needed something, a lesson in manners first of all. But in a situation like this, it was best for Jacob to keep a cool head.

"No, I can't say that we've met, have we?" he said casually, his fingers tightening over Kendall's arm, all the while thinking that his face did seem familiar.

The curly haired man grinned menacingly at Jacob, his cold, light-blue eyes boring into him.

Behind Jacob, a man cleared his throat. "That's Bob Stone," he whispered.

Jacob didn't turn or acknowledge the speaker but kept his stare on the man opposite him. Bob Stone. Robert Stone? Elliott "Slippery" Stone's older brother and the second in command of the Slippery Stone Gang?

Jacob almost wanted to laugh. Even in his shock he could recognize the truth.

It wasn't Elliott that brought Clifford Pierce to Valencia; it was Bob. To be perfectly honest, maybe that strategy was smarter. It was a longer way of getting to the head, but maybe more efficient. Take down the system around the gang leader as a way to finally get to him.

"Bob Stone, huh?" Jacob said, smiling back. "Pleased to meet you. Strange I didn't recognize you. Now you mention it, though, you look just like your brother."

"More handsome, though," he said, not dropping his gaze.

Jacob laughed. "I seem to recall that there are men looking for you, too. You'll have to come with me as well."

To himself, Jacob thought hell would have frozen over if he somehow managed to capture both Kendall and Stone in this moment, but he wasn't going to back down without trying. He stood up even straighter, using every inch of his breadth to intimidate.

"No. I don't think we'll be doing that," Stone said.

"We? Who else you got with ya, eh, Stone? Otis the Ox? Or Kansas City Cooper, maybe?

Who? Your brother around here? Seems I got a list of your known accomplices somewhere."

"So cocky, aren't you? I bet you're just like that other one. All talk, no action. You think just because you got your hand on a lowlife like that one that you're invincible."

"What other one?" Jacob asked, all mocking from his tone now. Did he mean Clifford Pierce?

Stone laughed. "This has been ... enlightening and all, but I'm afraid we have to get going. I appreciate you breaking up the fight though. My temper can get the best of me sometimes."

"You're going nowhere, Stone. You're coming with me," Jacob said again.

Without taking his eyes off the bounty hunter, Stone whistled and held his right hand out from his side. In an instant, a pistol was tossed directly into that hand from some accomplice in the crowd that Jacob hadn't noticed.

Before Jacob could react, Stone fired two shots at him. At the crowd. Jacob twisted and ducked away from the bullets, dropping Kendall in the process. He felt one of the bullets graze his upper arm, burning through his shirt and cutting the skin, but continuing on. The yells and cries of the men all around him filled the air.

Jacob recovered his feet under him and spun around to face Stone again, drawing his revolver as he did. He cursed himself for thinking this would be an easy capture of a drunk outlaw. He should have had his gun ready the whole time—he could have shot back at Stone immediately.

But Stone was gone.

He had shot into the crowd and disappeared.

Jacob looked around frantically, over the heads of the men yelling and pushing each other to get out of the way. No one wanted to be in the middle of a mob when shots were fired indiscriminately. Quick draw was one thing. Getting shot in the back by an anonymous foe was quite another.

In all the mayhem, Jacob had time to spare a thought for Pastor McGorry. Hopefully the good man had taken his own advice and gotten far away from the danger before the shooting began.

As that thought passed his mind, Jacob turned again to grab for Ross Kendall. The man had been unconscious and helpless when he was dropped into the dirt. He should be there still, and Jacob didn't want to be the reason the man got trampled in the panic.

But, no. Kendall was gone too.

Jacob spotted another man in a black duster, and he felt a pang of hope, but the fellow's long stringy blond hair told Jacob that wasn't his man.

Now, Jacob's heart started pounding. The adrenaline of the hunt coursed through him.

Where could he have gone?

He couldn't have gone far, not under his own power at least.

Jacob pushed through the crowd, not caring if he knocked a man over or accidentally stepped on someone's foot. Any minor injuries were nothing in the face of losing an outlaw who could be of danger to other people. Sure, Ross Kendall seemed to be a useless sort, but that didn't mean that letting him stay on the run was the answer.

Jacob pushed against the tide, getting an elbow to the ribs as he worked his way through the mass of men. Truly every resident of Valencia must be in that throng tonight.

When he finally got to the edge of the group, as it started to thin, Jacob's heart pounded even more. He had just picked a direction to follow, on a guess that Stone and Kendall would be trying to escape town altogether, but now that he had reached that edge he found nothing.

There were no tracks that stood out, no visuals along the horizon. Granted, it was after sunset, but the moon was still half waned and offered some light across the desert. And yet, still, Jacob had nothing to go on.

He didn't even know if Stone and Kendall had left the mess together. Maybe Jacob would have to go two different directions to find them. Maybe he'd never find them. Maybe they were already on horses and halfway to Mexico.

He continued his rapid pacing to the edge of town, to where the road led up out of the gathering of tents and into the hills. To where the miners traveled every morning at dawn to go seek their fortune.

The sounds of the town faded behind him, the farther into the hills Jacob walked. The light from the men's lanterns faded with it, and soon Jacob found his steps lit only by the moon and stars.

This was futile. This was pointless. He had just chosen this path at random and for all he knew this was taking him farther from the trails of either outlaw. He would have to regroup and start again in the morning.

He stopped, took a deep breath and tried to reason his way out of this.

It wasn't over. Not yet.

When he turned and looked down the hill back toward Valencia, Jacob felt a surge of fury and frustration welling up in him. He had had him. His hand had been around Kendall's arm. He had Stone right in front of him. And he had failed. He had lost them both.

Without regard to the desert fauna coming out of their burrows for the evening, Jacob yelled, a deep, guttural cry of defeat into the night sky.

CHAPTER NINE

"Good morning, Mr. Payne," Wes Beasley said, smiling up at the bounty hunter. The shopkeeper and Jacob's host was bent over the fire, feeding it small chips to keep the low burn going as a pot of coffee was being brought to boil over it. "Sleep well?"

Jacob stretched and nodded. He put a hand to his side where a bruise was forming. The crush of men in the chaos last night had pressed any number of sharp elbows into him, but it was an injury not even worth mentioning. The minor cut on his upper arm was already bandaged and Jacob could almost forget it had occurred.

"I'm mighty grateful to you and your brother," Jacob said. "I'm sure you can imagine, I've spent many a night on the hard dirt, so anytime I get something better I'm grateful. Last night I just slept like a baby."

"Good thing, too, if you're gonna do all you claimed last night." He pulled the coffee off the fire and poured a tin mug full. He handed it over to Jacob along with a hard biscuit. "Bacon is coming. Start with that to wake you up."

"Thank you," Jacob murmured. "You're right, though. I got a lot that I need to take care of today. Both of those men last night are wanted in Tucson, if not other places. I have to think they're still near enough that I can get my hands on them."

"So you were saying. And you know, since you mentioned it, Raymond and I have been talking."

"Oh?" Jacob asked through a mouthful of biscuit.

"You said that curly haired fellow is named Stone? That's not what we know him as. He's been a customer here for the last week at least. Maybe longer. Goes by the name Beauregard."

"The name he uses don't matter much. But he's been here a week, you say?"

"At least. I think longer, but I wouldn't swear to it." Wes began slicing off thick strips of bacon and dropping them in the already hot pan. "He's pretty tight-lipped. Won't answer direct questions and the like, but he can't keep secret the things he's been buying."

"And he's buying them, as well. Not stealing them?" Jacob clarified. "That also points to him wanting to keep a low profile."

"Exactly," Wes agreed. "As I say, Raymond and I compared notes, and this man we know as Beauregard has bought nearly everything a man could want for panning gold. Now, I don't know that he has a claim or if he been meaning to jump one, but at the very least it seems as though he'd been planning to stick around for a while."

"So you don't think he's the kind of man that would just up and leave all that? Even to escape capture? He is Slippery Stone's brother, after all."

"That's true." Wes rubbed his chin as he watched the bacon sizzle. "That's very true."

"There's no telling what a man like that will do," a new voice added. "Can't trust 'em. Can't trust a one of 'em."

A man who must have been Raymond Beasley staggered out of the sleeping tent, buttoning up his pants over his longjohns. Wes handed him a cup of coffee wordlessly, and the taller brother continued his rant.

"That's why we need the law in this town," he insisted fervently, as though Jacob would think to disagree. "Men come in here using fake names, and then shooting into a crowd of onlookers and then disappearing. It ain't right."

"You interested in helping me find him?" Jacob asked.

Raymond looked at his brother who rolled his eyes as he sat on a log near the fire. "Gotta talk to the wife," he said in a carrying whisper. "Miss Wes here don't like me going too far away from home. She gets scared."

"I'm not scared, Raymond Beasley," he said, irritated. "It's just that someone has to keep an eye on the wares and I can't be here every second. It's not like we have a door we can lock just yet."

"We'll get someone to help," Raymond said dismissively.

"We can't afford to get someone."

"We can now we got a paying boarder."

Both brothers looked at Jacob as though suddenly remembering that he was there.

"Oh. Well. That's true," Wes said.

"We'll find someone honest and dedicated and— Well, speak of the devil," Raymond concluded, standing to greet their new visitor.

"Pastor McGorry, I was just put in mind of you."

"Were you? How very flattering. I'm so sorry to disturb your breakfast boys—no, no coffee for me, thanks—but Mr. Payne I just wanted to come over and see how you were getting by this morning after throwing yourself in the midst of those ruffians last night?"

"I'm doing fine," Jacob said. "Just fine. Got a bruised rib for my trouble, and am no closer to capturing those outlaws, but I'll survive."

"Do you now? And do you think you might be further away from capturing the outlaws than you would have been if you had stayed out of it last night?"

"I— " Jacob opened his mouth to protest and then closed it again. He was completely surprised out of conversation.

Pastor McGorry moved on without waiting. "I actually came by to see if I could purchase some candles from you boys. As soon as you're ready to start business for the day. I have a mind to get up the next set of studs by sunset and want to get started and might be needing some light in order to finish."

"We'd be happy to," Raymond said, standing. "I'll take you over there now. In fact, I've been meaning to talk to you about a trade if you're amenable. See, we need a third man around here every so often..."

The conversation faded into the background as Raymond led the pastor to the tent full of hardware and supplies. Wes and Jacob sat silently together for a moment, each chewing on a couple slices of bacon and deep in their own thoughts.

"Huh," said Wes, a few moments after the pastor had gone. "Never thought I'd hear a man of the cloth so hellbent on saying 'I told you so.'"

Jacob caught his eye and couldn't help but laugh.

"Ah, but he's right, though. I'm certainly no closer to catching Kendall than I was yesterday, and might even be further away."

"You'll get him. And though Valencia seems to be full of outlaws, I'm certain there are some good, honest men around here too. We just have to find them."

"That reminds me," Jacob said, helping himself to a refill of coffee. "I heard about another bounty hunter coming out this way and I wonder if you've seen him. Clifford Pierce? Sorry, I've never met the man, so I couldn't tell you what he looks like."

Wes finished chewing his mouthful of bacon

while he thought. "The name sounds a mite familiar. When Ray is done— Oh! Ray, you remember that fellow was here a couple days ago? Was his name Clifford?"

Raymond walked past his brother, past the fire and ducked his head into the sleeping tent. When he came out, he was pulling on his shirt.

"You're all set, brother. The pastor will come over at midday or so to relieve you for a little while. I let him take a half-dozen candles free of charge for his trouble. Will that do you?"

Wes shrugged. "I'll make do. But what about this Clifford? He's a bounty hunter, and Jacob heard he come out this way."

Raymond grabbed a plate of bacon and stood while eating. "Clifford. Yeah, that sounds right," he said with his mouth full. "We sold him a rope, if I recall."

"Don't suppose he said anything to you about where he was going or what he'd be doing did you?" Jacob asked. "I know it's unlikely."

Raymond chewed more, while Wes began heating water over the stove and pulling out his shaving kit.

"Nothing specific. Just that he expected to stay in town a few days. Wonder why he didn't need a bed to stay in. You know, now's you mention it I'm sure I also saw him at the

Watering Hole night before last. Chatting up the other men and whatnot. Makes sense if he's also a bounty hunter, I guess, right?"

Jacob nodded. His competitive edge began to surface. It's not as though he wanted to stop this Pierce person from doing his job, but if Jacob could get to the outlaws first he was going to.

"Right, then. I'm going to the Watering Hole to see what I can find. I got two men on the run today and I can't waste another minute."

"Wait a second, I'll come with you."

Raymond stuffed another piece of bacon in his mouth with one hand and caught up his hat with the other. Pausing a second to grab his belt and holster, Raymond fastened his buckle while hurrying after the bounty hunter.

"You come back for supper, I'm fixing quail," Wes called after them as he began to lather his face with soap.

CHAPTER TEN

Even that early in the morning, the Watering Hole had plenty of customers. Several men leaned on their elbows at the makeshift bar, albeit drinking coffcc alongside their rye. More men sat scattered at tables around the tent. Jacob stood just inside the doorway to take in the scene. Other than the two outlaws he was after and the pastor, there wasn't any other man in Valencia that he knew. But he stored away the details of the men sitting in here, just in case he'd need them in the future.

Back in the far corner sat a group of four, three of the men seeming to hang on every word of the last. This man holding their attention seemed otherwise unremarkable. Average height, no distinguishing characteristics, hair the same ashy brown as thousands of others, and seemed to have gone without a shave for a few days. What could he be saying to them?

"There," Raymond said quietly pointing to the man holding court in the corner of the tent. "That's him. Clifford something or other that bought rope from us the other day."

"Really?"

Clifford Pierce, jawing with the locals? From all he had heard, that sounded about right. Jacob made his way across the room with Raymond following closely behind.

"Keep your mouth shut and listen," Jacob instructed his companion. "We don't want them to know what we want right off the bat."

Raymond nodded and shut his mouth tight, still following at Jacob's elbow.

Jacob plastered his face with an interested smile and made his way to Clifford's table. Any man that fond of hearing himself talk might not be too particular about what he says or who is listening.

"... And then I wrapped one hand over the man's throat," he was saying as Jacob and Raymond walked up. He held up one of his average-looking hands for his listeners to admire and paused dramatically. "I said 'drop it,' squeezing my fingers to emphasize my point, you see."

"What happened next?" one of the men asked.

Jacob forced himself to seem interested in the story as well, knowing full well that even if it were true in its essence, it must be embellished in its details.

"He did exactly as I said. And he told his partner to do the same. There's not many a bounty hunter in this area that can bring down two infamous characters like those two without shedding a drop of blood."

"But you did." The speaker couldn't be more than seventeen, Jacob thought, just lapping up all these tales.

"I did," Clifford said with a solemn nod.

"Who else've you captured, Cliff?" the kid asked excitedly.

"Oh, now, let's see," the bounty hunter said, leaning back in his chair. He took a sip of his whiskey, pretending to think, and rested his feet up on the table. Dust fell onto the tabletop, and the men closest to him surreptitiously moved their own cups out of the way.

"Benny Jones, outta St. Louis. Mac Bohannon. His partner, you might not've heard of, but Hector Rivera."

"Geez," the kid said.

"A few others too. In fact, I seem to have run through most of the jobs around here. Not much left but the biggest names, and I heard someone say that Slippery Stone himself was out this way. So, packed up my trusty steed Sugar"—when he grinned, Jacob noticed he was missing one of his eye teeth—"and came out this way."

"Slippery Stone?" one of the other men asked in awe.

Clifford nodded. "When I got here, I learned it was actually his brother Bob, but one Stone is almost as good as the other. The bounty on his head is almost as large.

"And now after that display we had last night, I learned we got not one, but *two* known outlaws around town. Not to mention that head honcho's accomplices. I bet they're someone. Bet there's a nice fat bounty on their heads as well, and I aim to get me some."

"You know what that one guy did?" one of the men asks. "The one that almost got beaten up last night?"

Clifford shook his head. "Dunno. Sure he deserved that beating, though."

"I'll get that man," Raymond said over the

murmurs. "I'll get my hands on him and bring him to justice."

"You still campaigning, Beasley?" another man called out.

"Valencia needs a sheriff," he insisted. "Someone who knows the industry of all the men who live here."

"Yeah yeah," the heckler said. "We've heard it all."

"This is why I'm glad you're accepting my help," Ray said to Jacob, under his breath. "Seems nothing is gonna get through to these boys but results."

Jacob nodded but kept his mouth shut.

"How you think you're gonna get 'em?" the kid asked.

Jacob silently blessed the young man for his pointed questions. There was nothing better for getting a vain man to talk than good old hero worship.

"Oh, I saw where they went off to last night. Later today I'll go out there and just collect 'em." Clifford shrugged nonchalantly as though capturing one of the most infamous outlaws in the territory was no big deal.

"You know where that fellow disappeared to?" Jacob asked, trying to keep his tone of innocent wondering.

"Sure do. You know a lot of things when you wait and watch."

Jacob refrained himself from rolling his eyes at the condescension.

"But it seemed like he just disappeared," one of the seated men said eagerly. "Did Stone help him?"

Clifford shook his head. "No. Well, yes, but not much. There were those shots, right? Then Stone made some gesture and a couple other boys scooped up the drunk one. Kendall, I think his name is. Think that's what I heard from where I was standing. And they dragged the man straight back between the tents to the foot of the hill."

Jacob held his breath, hoping that Clifford would reveal all he knew.

"I followed him out of the herd, last night, up into the hills. I didn't have my rope on me at the time, since I'd been in here with you lot. I watched him curl up in a little cave not thirty feet off the main path, and I just let him go. But I'm not worried. With as drunk as that boy was last night he's apt to be still sleeping it off. He can set for another few hours while I enjoy my morning."

"I think that's all we need to hear," Jacob

said in a low voice to Raymond. "Let's go get him."

He hadn't been quiet enough, however. Just as Jacob turned to go, he heard the other bounty hunter call for him to wait.

"You're not going after my bounty, are you?" Clifford asked, a threat in his tone.

Jacob turned around to eye the man, who hadn't even deigned to stand when challenging him.

"Hey ... You. I recognize you now that I get a good look at you. You're that one that tried to arrest him last night and failed, ain't ya? I come in to clean up your mess and you're going to screw me over?"

Jacob seethed. He was done with this man.

"First of all, it's *my* bounty. You didn't even know about it till I got to town. You don't even know what he's wanted for."

Clifford shrugged. "Can't be that hard to figure out once I take him back to Tucson."

"Second of all, I'm just doing my job, while you sit around twiddling your thumbs. Maybe you're such a legend in the territory because you've got a couple big names but I don't see any of that action now. Now I just see a man too interested in drinking and praising himself to capture an outlaw who was just laying down in front of him."

The other bounty hunter stood now, staring down Jacob.

"Third of all," Jacob continued without fear, "I also intend to get my hands on Bob Stone. If you're lucky, maybe I'll hire you to help guard both men on my way back to Tucson."

"You watch your mouth. I'm not even going to bother trying to beat you to him. I know what I know. And I know that I'm the only man that's going to be able to catch this Kendall fellow, especially if he's in league with Stone. I'll just wait and watch you hang yourself."

Jacob scoffed. Such arrogance from someone who'd been drinking first thing in the morning.

"All right then. You have a good day, now."

Jacob tipped his hat and started his way out of the Watering Hole, the eyes of all the other patrons on him.

Behind him he heard Raymond get in one last word before following Jacob to the door.

"And when I help this man capture the outlaw, I hope you'll remember my name when it comes time to vote for sheriff of this place."

CHAPTER ELEVEN

Jacob waited in the street outside the Watering Hole for Raymond to catch up with him. He turned over the details in his mind, trying to remember the exact wording Clifford had used when describing where Ross Kendall had crawled off to. He would have to go back to where he left his pack in the Beasley brothers' tent to collect his own rope, and maybe extra ammunition. Just in case.

"Well, that just beat all, don't it?" Ray said as he exited the tent. "Who woulda thought he'd just come right out and tell you where to find the outlaw?"

Jacob grinned. "Oh, I've known men like him before. My father, as a matter of fact. You ask the right questions and can get anything you want out of them. Just so they can be the one to say it."

Ray laughed. "You're right. Come to think about it, I think the reverend back at our home in Georgia did the same."

"And now we've gotten what we need out of him, it's time for the hard part. You sure you want to help with this part, Ray? It's not going to be easy, and it's probably going to be dangerous."

"I'm sure. You gotta go back to the tent anyway, right? Let's just check once more to make sure Wes ain't got his knickers in a bunch before I agree to this deadly adventure."

Back at the Beasley brothers' camp, Wes was helping a customer pick out a shovel while Pastor McGorry stood looking through the empty burlap sacks.

"You boys are back already?" the pastor said.

"You're here to work already?" Raymond asked.

"I forgot I needed one of these," he said. "And I figured you'd be gone most of the day, helping this law man." He gestured at Jacob with a smile. "Any way I can help, I'm happy to. The wall can go up tomorrow just as well."

Jacob left the men to talk while he went back to the sleeping tent to collect what he needed. He knew where he should be able to find Ross Kendall. That was one. That might have to be enough, but if he saw the opportunity to go after Bob Stone, he certainly wouldn't let it go. He measured out the rope he had with him: only one length. He'd have to buy more from the Beasleys. He checked his gun, his bullets, his bandage. He was as ready as he would ever be.

When he went back out to the hardware store and asked Wes for another length of rope, he took the opportunity to ask Ray about the cave where they were heading.

"Are you familiar with it? If Kendall walked up there on his own, I don't need to be bringing my horse, do I?"

"Nah," Ray said as he unholstered his own gun and checked the chamber to see how many bullets it held. "It's not far. Maybe half a mile up and a few yards off the trail. It's the kind of place partway between the mining fields and the town where a man might go catch a nap after working all day and night. It's really nothing. Barely a hole. If Kendall has been in town a while, that might be how he knows of it."

In short order, both men were as equipped as they needed to be, with hats pulled low over their faces to protect from the sun. Raymond led the way out of Valencia, toward the trail that led up to the hills and to the gold.

"You and Wes not planning to mine at all?" Jacob asked. "Seems like a good opportunity since you're here already."

"I might," Raymond said. "But Wes is adamant that we'll make more money with the store. Higher reward for less risk, is what he keeps saying. He just don't want me spending thousands on a claim, I think. If the right opportunity came along I'd give it a shot. But— have you ever panned for gold?"

Jacob shook his head.

"It's hard work. In water or on your knees all day. Your eyes go just about crossed staring at the same patch of dirt and water, just hunting for a tiny glimpse of gold flake. Sure, some men fall on a load of nuggets, but those are few and far between. It's far more likely that you'd spend a week of twenty-hour days for about ten dollars of gold dust. No, I think Wes has the right idea. Sell those men the shovels instead."

That sentiment made sense to Jacob. He wished them well. Those Beasleys seemed like good men, and Ray would make an excellent sheriff whenever the town got around to incorporating properly. With him leading the political landscape and McGorry leading the spiritual, this might just be one of the few boom towns that managed to keep itself from descending into bedlam.

Jacob smiled to himself, wondering if he'd be coming back to Valencia after a bounty any time soon.

On their way up the hill, the two men passed a pair of enormous boulders a few yards off the trail. Jacob couldn't say why the formation caught his eye. It seemed to be a stone face built into the side of the hill. He wanted to hurry up to the cave to get to Kendall before the man woke up and realized he might be in danger. But Jacob made a mental note to check on the boulders on his way back down the hill, when his prey was already secured.

"Here's the turn off," Ray said a few moments later. He pointed to a narrow path between the shrubs on the left side of the main trail. Jacob might have missed it if he hadn't known to look for it.

"Just straight down this way?" Jacob said, his voice lowered.

Ray nodded.

"I'll lead," the bounty hunter directed. "You cover my back, and keep an eye out for anyone else coming up the trail. Kinda surprised we haven't run into Clifford Pierce already to be honest."

Ray nodded again, unholstered his gun and followed in Jacob's footsteps.

The cave Clifford had described was about twenty yards ahead, cut into the hill where thousands of years ago water had carved it out. Even from several feet away, Jacob could tell that it was a shallow cave, only maybe a dozen feet deep. It wasn't any kind of real hideout or useful for anything other than an afternoon nap. Perhaps the natives may have used this cool hole for storage, but evidently none lived nearby any longer, so the white man had taken it over for his own selfish deeds.

Just as Clifford had described, a small, bearded man in a black duster, lay curled up on the floor of the cave, deep in the shade, snoring like a bear.

Jacob was gratified that he wasn't too late. There was a fear that the other bounty hunter might get in his way, but now Jacob knew that he was right to come after this man. This would be an easy capture. He'd take Kendall back to Tucson, collect the bounty, and there would be one fewer monster loose to harass the good men and women of Arizona.

In a whisper, Jacob described to Raymond

what they would do, what role each man had, and what to expect. The aspiring sheriff listened and nodded seriously. He seemed determined to not be a liability.

As one, the men crept forward to the cave. Ross Kendall had cornered himself.

The first thing Jacob did when he got near enough was to reach forward and ever so gently remove the revolver from Kendall's holster. The way he was laying, the gun sat almost casually balanced on the man's left hip. He may have another gun crammed somewhere underneath his body, but Jacob wanted to be sure Kendall was bound before he woke.

After handing the revolver to Ray, Jacob then slowly, gently looped his rope around the man's head and shoulders. He couldn't push it down low enough to pin Kendall's arms to his side; but if he pulled the rope tightly where it was, he'd be creating a noose.

Hoping for the best, Jacob crouched down behind the sleeping outlaw, wedged his hand under the man's shoulder and hauled him to sitting up. With one motion he both moved the man to upright and lowered the rope to be taut against his torso. Quickly, the loop was tightened before Kendall was even awake enough to realize what was happening.

"There now," Jacob said, roughly. "You're under arrest. As I said last night. And this time you're not getting away."

Kendall was awake now—enough to let loose a string of curses that set Ray to laughing.

"That's it?" Raymond asked. "That's being a bounty hunter? That seems awful easy."

Jacob laughed. "They're not all this easy, but to be sure the whiskey and the beating he got last night helped. If you're thinking about becoming a bounty hunter instead of a sheriff, you should come with me on a harder job some-time. This isn't enough of a good example."

Ray nodded. He held his own gun pointed at the still stumbling outlaw while Jacob hauled him to his feet. "I might. Seems like fun and adventure."

CHAPTER TWELVE

Ray was laughing and joking with Kendall as the three made their way back to the main trail to head back into town. Stepping between shrubs, Ray would alternate pushing Kendall ahead of him and then hurrying to catch up to continue his harassment. The outlaw took it all without much complaint. He was sullen but not angry. It was almost as though he had given up a while ago and seemed to have accepted his fate pretty quickly.

"You're gonna help me get elected sheriff," Ray was saying. "I'm gonna make sure the folks down in Valencia see you all tied up like this."

Mentally, Jacob was planning the rest of his time there in Valencia, wondering if there was somewhere he could leave Ross Kendall under lock and key while he continued his search for Bob Stone. If only Valencia had just one finished structure. Since he was on this side of the state where the outlaw was last seen, he had to at least try. Getting one of the Slippery Stone Gang was always priority. He wondered if Stone was even still in town, though. Maybe he had run when he knew a bounty hunter was also here. This job hadn't turned out exactly as he expected, but maybe it could end even better.

As they walked, Jacob wrestled with himself over how he would feel if that pompous fool Clifford Pierce nabbed Stone instead. It felt like the outlaw was almost within his grasp—just as he had felt a few weeks ago when Jacob spotted his brother in Tucson. The choice the bounty hunter had had to make that day still haunted him. He had to watch the most wanted outlaw in the territory just run away from him while he stayed put.

Jacob felt like a failure that day. And many of the days since. He was getting over it now— that was part of the reason he had ended his convalescence early. He could admit that now. But today, faced with a similar choice he realized he would have to go after Bob Stone. He prayed the opportunity presented itself.

Jacob still had a two-day ride back to

Tucson, and there was no town big enough between here and there to turn any outlaws over to the law. He'd have to take Kendall—and maybe, hopefully, Stone—all the way back to Santos.

Jacob was mostly listening to Ray's bantering, but was distracted by another noise he heard underneath it, in the distance. It seemed almost like an echo, but where they were on the hill seemed to just open up to the valley beyond. Where could that sound be coming from?

Jacob stopped walking. He put his hand up to Ray to indicate he should halt too. Ray saw the look on the bounty hunter's face and quit speaking abruptly. They were out in the open; Jacob glanced around for some cover.

"What's happening?" Kendall whined. "I thought we were going. I'm hungry."

"Hush," Ray said coldly. "You're lucky we haven't gagged you yet."

The outlaw hushed, but glared at the other two.

Jacob handed over the lead rope to Ray so his hands could be free, but kept the other length of rope looped over his shoulder.

"Stay here," he whispered. "Keep your eyes open. Maybe get cover." He slowly crept slightly farther down the hill. It was just a guess, but it seemed like this was where the sound was coming from.

Jacob sniffed the air, just in case there was some clue, some smell that would tell him what he was walking in to. All he could pick out was the sweaty, stale scent of an unwashed man. But, given there were two of those standing on the trail behind him, Jacob couldn't put much stock in that. He sniffed again. Maybe something else. Something faint. But whatever it was was too far away.

He heard the same sound. This time it sounded more human than before. A muffled, rustling, frustrated sound.

Jacob turned slowly toward the opposite side of the trail. He had an inkling what it was. He had certainly heard sounds like that before. But he hoped he was wrong.

His weapon was already in his hand.

When they had walked up toward where Ross Kendall was hiding, the big stones wedged into the side of the hill just seemed like part of the landscape. It appeared as some gigantic steps or carved formation that were part of the low mountain from centuries earlier.

Coming at them from this angle, however, Jacob realized they weren't quite as dug deeply into the plane as he had thought. Ten or fifteen feet tall and almost right on top of one another, the boulders were a good thirty feet off the main trail. Shrubs and weeds peppered the hillside, among smaller boulders. It didn't look at all the same from here. Coming downhill a body had to really know to look for them.

But because Jacob thought he had heard something, he thought to look for them.

He looked back to Ray who frowned at him, confused. Whatever Jacob may be about to find would be news to the citizens of Valencia. Not a man had mentioned any hint of these boulders when he had been asking.

He crept closer to the boulders, closer, holding his breath to stay as quiet as possible. The rustling, mumbling sound seemed louder the closer he got to them. But not just louder. Louder and slightly echoing.

That echoing, hollow noise went against all the other evidence of his senses. If someone had asked him twenty minutes ago, he would have sworn that these two giant boulders crammed together against the hill were all there was. Smashed tightly by nature.

But now, with the sounds reverberating, with that heretofore unnoticed dark gap near the top, and with the now-unmistakable smell of a campfire, Jacob had other suspicions.

He reached the boulders, now so far off the path that he could no longer see Ray and their prisoner. Jacob walked the perimeter, around the curve of the boulders that stood out from the dirt. He sniffed again. He peered up at the gap made where the rocks curved away from each other at the top.

It was difficult for his eyes to pick out, but his nose did not mistake it—smoke. There was a campfire nearby.

Jacob bent down to examine the gap where the rocks curved at the bottom and found it crammed full of weeds and shrubs. The dirt had filled in the space through the rain and storms, plants taking hold and overrunning the space.

But at the top ...

At the top was a gap that rang of possibility. But how to get up there. This near the boulder, the hill's incline was awfully steep, but if he just—

Jacob holstered his gun reluctantly. He would need both hands to climb up the side of the hill and get to the top of the rock. He couldn't ask Ray to just leave Kendall and watch his back. He couldn't make the climb with only one hand. He had to risk it and hope that he didn't run into anyone or anything that would make him regret being unarmed.

When he grabbed for one of the sturdier-looking shrubs in the hill above his head, the dirt and pebbles packed around the plant's roots rained down on his face. Jacob blinked, trying to keep dust out of his eyes. He wiped his eyes with the back of his other hand and tried again. With a tentative tug, Jacob determined that the bush might just hold him, or at least help him keep his balance once he found a foothold.

Jacob took a deep breath and dug the toe of one boot into the side of the hill. Holding on to the stalk above him, he pulled himself up that first step. He leaned flat against the dirt.

It held.

He tried again, a second step, using the point of his boot to gain leverage in the soft dirt, and laying as close against the incline as he could. Slowly, step by awkward, dirty step, Jacob crawled his way up the side of the hill, up the side of the boulder. After several long, filthy minutes of all but lying in the dirt, the bounty hunter found himself able to scramble to the top of the closest boulder.

He heard his boots scrape against the stone and winced. Whoever or whatever was nearby would have been able to hear that if they were listening hard enough. As soon as he was settled and balanced in a sitting position, precarious though it may be, Jacob drew his weapon.

Just to his left, about three feet off and down, was a gap. Not a gap—a veritable opening into a cave beyond. A cave that until that moment Jacob had no idea existed. Anyone walking up the hill to the gold fields would have assumed these stones were simply part of the solid hill, but now that he was closer, Jacob had found an opening to a cave buried deep inside.

And now, sitting near the opening, he confirmed he had been right in his suspicions. Somewhere deep in that hidden cave was a campfire. He didn't smell any food, but the unmistakable scent of wood burning was potent. Smoke was escaping through this gap between the boulders.

There was absolutely no mistaking it.

And over the sound of the campfire, echoed through the darkness, a man was talking. A man whose voice Jacob recognized.

"I know you thought you'd get your hands on me," Bob Stone said, "but now look who's captured."

CHAPTER THIRTEEN

Jacob could have kicked himself. Of course the notorious outlaw would have found this hide-out. If there was a secret, protected corner of the town, the worst men would find a way to exploit it. Of course Stone had found a place to run to. How did Jacob not see this coming?

And he had somehow managed to drag a prisoner down here with him.

A muffled protest answered Stone's threat. The outlaw laughed.

"Yep, keep yelling. No one is going to hear you all the way out here. This will teach you to mess with things you can't handle. You thought you'd be a big man, I bet. Big man from the big city come to show me what's what."

More muffled cries.

Jacob had to do something. He couldn't look down into the cave without being seen himself. If he leaned into the opening he'd be in full silhouette, blocking the likely only natural light Stone and his prisoner had. While he debated his next step, Jacob listened more. He needed to determine if Stone was the only one of his gang in there.

After several minutes of no further noises, Jacob made a decision. He didn't want to be walking into a battle but he hadn't heard but the one set of footsteps. In Stone's arrogance and self-importance, he had left himself just this little bit vulnerable. No doubt he had tasked his men with something elsewhere, as he holed up in what he imagined to be safety.

Jacob formulated a plan as he scrambled back down to the ground and out to the trail where Ray waited.

"You see something?" the man asked in a loud whisper.

Jacob nodded as he ran the final steps.

"There's a cave back there."

The shock on Ray's face almost made Jacob laugh. "Like hell."

"I'm telling you. It's almost completely hidden, from this side at least, but it's a bonafide hideout for the man that can find it. And you'll never guess who found it."

Ray looked blank for a split second before blurting out, "Stone?"

"Sounds like it," Jacob said with a nod. "I didn't lay eyes on him, but heard him threatening someone. Someone gagged."

"Who?"

"Don't know. Sounded like a man, but that's as much as I could tell. Whoever it was made the mistake of threatening Stone, or something." Jacob took a deep breath. "We can't leave him."

"Are you sure?" Ray peered around the bounty hunter to look toward the boulders and the minuscule gap again. "Is tussling with Bob Stone over the fate of someone we don't even know the best idea? We could go back to town to get reinforcements."

"And risk missing our chance? Would the sheriff of Valencia leave a man in such straits?"

Ray grinned. "All right. You're right. Tell me what we're going to do."

Jacob laid out the details—sparse, as he couldn't rightly make much plan without seeing the layout of the cave and what all they were facing—and then hurried back to climb up the boulder. While he did that, Ray took the cowering Ross Kendall almost all the way down the hill to a tall cottonwood tree that stood just a bit off the trail. He had described it all to Jacob, assuring him the tree was sturdy enough and secluded enough, that Kendall would be still tied up there when they got through dealing with Stone.

To himself, Jacob wondered if the outlaw had enough gumption or will to even try to escape now that he was already bound, but the safer he stayed the better.

While waiting for Ray to return, Jacob had time to do more listening and more reconnaissance. Sitting atop the boulder, his ears trained on every rustle and rattle of the cave below, Jacob determined with some certainty that there was only one prisoner, and only the one outlaw. He couldn't be sure how far from him they were, but guessed not far, with the smoke from the campfire heading this way.

The cave seemed to be deep. So deep, in fact, that Jacob wondered if there was another opening on the other side of the hill. It sounded as though Stone walked away from his prisoner and the echoes of his boots on the hard ground grew fainter.

That would be his best chance. Jacob saw

Ray come around the bend in the trail, waved frantically to get his attention, then gestured.

He was going in.

He was taking this chance, this one moment when the outlaw might not be looking.

Might.

He had to risk it.

Jacob made sure his gun was holstered and his belt was tight. He slipped to the side, holding on to the edge of the boulder. His fingers tightened, forearms clenched as he lowered himself down and held his full weight with just his arms. Jacob straightened, getting as close to the ground as he could, then dropped the final five feet to the cave floor.

Through it all, he had remained silent, barring the thud when his boots met earth. As Jacob's eyes adjusted to the darkness, he heard a muffled burst of surprise, and turned toward the prisoner.

The prisoner. Even in such little light, Jacob recognized this man.

Eyes wide as he noticed Jacob, the bounty hunter Clifford Pierce sat against the side of the cave, against the packed dirt walls. His feet were bound at the ankles, his legs stretched in front of him. His hands were bound behind him, and he leaned forward, hunched over as though defeated.

Jacob was just as surprised to see him. His heart started hammering. Clifford Pierce was a man who had somehow managed to hunt down most of the biggest bounties in the area, and yet he had been overpowered and captured by Stone.

Jacob was about to hurry to the man's side before he remembered himself. He stopped. Listened. Footsteps in the distance were coming closer. He caught Clifford's eye, gestured to him to be quiet, and then backed up into the darkest corner of the cave, praying that Stone would not glance that way.

Clifford was only a few yards from where Jacob had entered. The campfire was another eight or ten feet past him, and the cave stretched out beyond even that. The light from the fire illuminated some of the space, but the dancing shadows made it hard for Jacob to identify anything beyond the immediate circle of light.

Where had Stone gone? How big was this cave? If only he could ask Clifford without them being overheard.

Jacob heard the faint scraping of boots outside the opening to the cave. Raymond must be near. Jacob wished he could have said just one word to the man. Either come this instant or wait it out. But there was nothing to be done about it now.

Clifford groaned into his gag and leaned back against the wall. Even in the dim light Jacob could see that his shirt was soaked through with blood. There was so much blood, in fact, over his right arm, chest and stomach that Jacob couldn't tell how the wounds had even occurred. How many bullet wounds could that be?

Jacob was about to see about staunching the blood when several things happened at once.

The scraping sound above him grew louder and the sunlight was blocked out. Raymond lowered himself into the cave, just as awkwardly as Jacob had and no less quiet. Jacob had to move a step farther away from Clifford to avoid being dropped on by his companion.

At the same time, the heavy footsteps returned from the other end of the cave. There was no chance to hide, barely an opportunity to draw his gun. A shadowed figure stopped on the other side of the fire, flames casting dancing light over his face.

"Who the— ?" Stone stammered, as soon as

he realized there were other figures in the cave with him.

Without any further word, the man dropped the small bundle he had been carrying and grabbed for his pistol.

"You're under arrest, Robert Stone," Jacob yelled, futilely, pointing his own weapon.

But the man had already begun shooting, albeit erratically.

The crack of gunshot echoed around him. Jacob couldn't tell how many shots were being fired or in what direction. He felt cornered, trapped, his back against the wall as a devil advanced.

From behind him, Jacob heard a cry of pain as Raymond registered a bullet wound.

"Hully gee!" the man swore.

Another crack of gunshot sounded. Jacob fired toward Stone, knowing his aim was wide. Jacob sensed a bullet just pass him. Another hit the dirt near his feet. Jacob moved, determined to not give the outlaw a stationary target in so small of a space. The stone wall behind him cracked with the impact of another shot.

He fired again at their attacker. Stone grunted, but with just the barest of campfire lights Jacob couldn't be sure where he was hit. Another shot. And another. But Stone had backed up, away, around the small bend of the cave and into the shadows. Jacob fired into the darkness.

Stone fired again. Clifford cried out, into his gag. Jacob clenched his teeth. He would have to make his move.

But suddenly, unexpectedly, all gunshots ceased. Stone had stopped firing. His trigger clicked on the empty chamber. He had run out of ammunition.

"Goddamn it!" Stone yelled.

The defiant yell echoed through the cave. He cursed again and jammed the useless weapon back in its holster.

The eyes of the two men met over the fire for only an instant before Stone turned and fled.

"No!" Jacob said. "STOP!"

The bounty hunter hesitated for one short moment. He had to make his choice. He could shoot that man in the back, risking his own reputation, the life of a—he had to admit—wonderful bounty hunter, and maybe the life of his new friend. Or he could let the devil go, save Clifford's life, save Raymond's, and be satisfied with the outlaw he had already captured.

All of this went through Jacob's mind in the blink of an eye.

Whose life was worth more? Whose safety

more assured? It was the same options he had had just a few weeks earlier when the man's brother had been seen in the streets of Tucson. The same choice that made Jacob doubt himself and his abilities.

But it was the same choice he had to make this time.

CHAPTER FOURTEEN

He made his decision. The only one he could make.

Jacob took the few steps to close the gap between the other bounty hunter and himself. In a quick movement, he had pulled his Bowie knife out of his boot and begun sawing at the ropes that bound Clifford Pierce.

In that choice—to save a decent man instead of pursuing a bad one—Bob Stone took his chance. Jacob could hear the outlaw's steps echoing farther away as he ran.

"Clifford. Can you hear me?"

He pulled down the man's gag. The other bounty hunter gasped and coughed at the sudden freedom. Jacob hacked through the rope binding the man's feet and asked again.

"Clifford?"

"Yes. Yes, I'm awake," he croaked. A low, husky groan tore out of him when Jacob moved him.

"I'm sorry," Jacob said, shuffling the man forward a few inches to get at the rope behind him. "This will just take a moment."

A quick sawing through the ropes around Clifford's wrists was all it took to free him.

"You've been shot," Jacob said. It wasn't a question.

Clifford was too weak to even nod.

He was alive. That was something. Jacob could assess the full damage in a moment.

He took a deep breath and stood up, turning to check on Ray immediately. The aspiring sheriff was also seated in the cave, with his back against the wall. He clutched his leg.

"I'm okay, Jacob. Tend to him. It's just my calf," he said grimly. "Bullet went straight through, but damn is that painful. Maybe I don't want to be the sheriff. This is why I sell hardware."

He winced, wrapping his fingers around his leg.

Jacob could laugh, grateful the man still had a sense of humor. He hesitated a moment, before Ray urged him on.

"Go. *Go!* You can still catch him."

Needing no further validation, Jacob abandoned them for the hunt.

In two steps he was darting through the darkness of the cave, off in the only direction the outlaw could have gone. His boots echoed against the rock as he ran blindly into the unknown. Past the campfire and Stone's dropped belongings, toward where he had seen the outlaw disappear.

He had to try. He had to run after Bob Stone. He couldn't just let this man get away from him the way his brother had. This time was different. This time Jacob wasn't injured nearly as badly as he had been on that day of the Tucson jailbreak.

There must be another entrance to the cave in that direction. Jacob cursed himself for not determining that sooner. He could have saved Ray the danger and posted him on that side. It was too late for what-ifs now. Jacob had two injured men on his hands and he had to save lives first and foremost.

But now he could give chase.

Those two weeks of rest paid off and Jacob sprinted into the darkness. After about twenty yards he began to see light ahead of him. It was faint at first but after another few steps, Jacob realized he was running toward daylight. It was another entrance to the cave. The exit through which Stone had likely disappeared.

Spurred on by this sight, Jacob dug in and ran even faster, darting around rocks and ruts in the cave floor. He no longer heard Stone's footsteps ahead of him, but that didn't mean he wasn't there.

He closed the final steps to the opening, a tall narrow crack between the hillside and another enormous boulder. Jacob had to slow down and turn sideways to shimmy through the space but he made it. As he stepped out into the sunlight on the hillside, he shaded his eyes, blinking, adjusting to the brightness.

Where had the man gone?

The bang of rifle sounded. The boulder behind him chipped, shards of stone flying, and Jacob ducked instinctively. A second gunshot cracked, and the dust at Jacob's feet bloomed in a cloud where it had been hit.

"Ya!" a man's voice called.

Jacob lowered his hand, looking toward the sound.

Halfway down the hill, between where Jacob stood and where the town of Valencia lay at the foot, stood four men on four horses, all but one aiming their guns in Jacob's direction. Another shot rang out, this one going well wide of Jacob into the hillside.

It seemed that killing him was not their goal, though why he couldn't say. A brief memory of Elliott Stone warning one of his men flashed through his mind.

Jacob began to run, toward the men, toward the outlaws, toward the immense bounty that could be waiting for him if he caught even one of these Slippery Stone Gang members.

But the minute he took a step forward, they were off, galloping down the hill in a wide circuit around the town and into the desert.

Jacob half-heartedly ran a few more steps before slowing to a stop. He was winded from his sprint and the adrenaline of two firefights. But even if he was not, he couldn't hope to catch up to them, even if Blaze was already saddled and waiting for him.

This was it.

He had failed.

Not completely, he reminded himself. He did still have Ross Kendall; he had hopefully saved the life of Clifford Pierce.

But Jacob himself would always remember this as the day that Bob Stone escaped him. Twice. Three times if you counted the previous evening.

Jacob groaned to himself. Three times.

He would get that man. Jacob swore to it. He would make it his aim to take down all of the Stones. It didn't matter who else was in the western frontier, Jacob Payne would be the bounty hunter to bring these men to justice.

Dejected and defeated, Jacob made his way back into the cave and to the two injured men. Clifford had to see a doctor, as soon as possible.

When he made it back to the campfire and the light, Ray was bent over Clifford but looked up at Jacob's footsteps.

"He get away?" He nodded. "Thought as much. A man like that isn't going to be caught too easily."

"He had his accomplices *and* all their horses outside the cave just waiting."

"Smart. That's what I'd do. That's what you'd do too, I reckon, isn't it?"

Jacob nodded. "He going to be all right?"

"I think so. We gotta get him into town though. When you left, I noticed Stone had dropped something in the dirt. Went to go see what it was and realized he was bringing a canteen of water and bandages to our friend here. I've done what I can, but we're still in a cave for christssake, aren't we?"

Jacob couldn't help but laugh. Men like this were the reason he couldn't stay in despair long.

"Let's get him out of here," Jacob agreed.

Between the two of them, they got Clifford to standing and propped him up between them. Jacob had to take most of the weight, Raymond limping his way through the cave to the other side, but the three men made their way out to the sunlight and down into Valencia in time for supper.

CHAPTER FIFTEEN

The men made their way down the hill, slowly, painfully, careful with every step to avoid making any injury worse. There was no doctor in Valencia yet, but one of the gold miners had been a medic in the war. He had some skill and could do his best for Clifford. Between the two of them, Ray and Jacob got the injured bounty hunter seen to. The miner who helped him counted four bullet holes, almost all in the man's torso, and predicted that if Ray hadn't been as prompt as he was in treating the injuries, he might not have made it.

Jacob worried about leaving the man in such a place like this. He would have to trust that Clifford could take care of himself, or that a man like Pastor McGorry might look out for him. Jacob himself had to many of his own problems to be dealing with.

Clifford was holding on to consciousness through all of this, and Jacob could see that he had things he wanted to say. This was neither the time nor the place for the two men to smooth over any animosities. He left the tent before Clifford could exert any more energy. There was still another loose end he had to take care of.

While Wes bandaged up his brother's leg, Jacob took the latter's directions and hiked back up the hill to where Ross Kendall waited, still tied to the cottonwood tree.

"Where you been?" he demanded angrily. "I got the worst headache. I gotta get out of the sun. I need a bite. You got water? You can't just abandon me in the wilderness like this."

Jacob said nothing to the man's complaints, but merely untied him wearily, checked that his wrists were still bound, and led the way back down the hill. The territory was much better off with this man captured. Jacob was willing to deal with such annoyances to keep other people safe. It could be so much worse.

Even so, he wished Kendall would stop talking.

"Where we going now? There ain't no sheriff

in this town. Where are you taking me? You know you could just let me go, right, fella? I ain't gonna do anything. I learned my less—"

Kendall was cut off in his protestations when he tripped over a large stone in the path. Jacob waited patiently for him to get to his feet again.

"You know if you weren't complaining so much you might have seen that in your path."

"Shut up," Kendall said. But then he remained silent the rest of the walk.

Reaching Valencia again, Jacob headed to the Beasley brothers' tents so he could make his good-byes. With still two full days to ride back, and plenty of daylight left, Jacob wanted to get started as soon as he could.

Pastor McGorry was still waiting around, helping out at the store where he could. When Jacob approached, he looked up eagerly. "You made it! Ray told us all about it, but I still wanted to stick around to see you with my own eyes."

"Yes, unfortunately, the other ones got away."

"You could let me get away too," Kendall said under his breath. "I won't tell no one."

"Ah, no matter," the pastor said dismissively.

"They're not in town any more from what I hear. We'll be better off without 'em."

"But if Stone has a gold claim, he'll be back."

"That's true. But he might not. Could be he had been waiting to jump someone else. Either way, the Lord works in mysterious ways and whatever will be will be. We'll just give thanks that all of you escaped with your life."

"Thanks to me," Ray said, limping up. "You heading out, Jacob? Don't you worry about your bill with my brother," he told him as Jacob pulled out his billfold. "I learned a lot from you. You saved this town from a mess of trouble. We'll call it even."

"Thank you, kindly. I sure do appreciate it. I'm happy to help any way I can."

"Just be sure you don't come this way again without stopping by. Next time you're here we'll even have a door."

"I'll do that," he said with a laugh. "You'll make a great sheriff. Your brother is a great shopkeeper and I think between the three of you this town will be quite the oasis for miners looking to make their fortune."

"Oh, we'll do all right. Take care that one don't fall off the horse when you're not looking."

With that final good-bye, Jacob set off

toward Tucson with Ross Kendall sitting on the saddle in front of him. The man would whine and complain the whole time about not getting his own ride, but in the end he lapsed into tired silence.

Jacob was disappointed that Bob Stone, second worst outlaw in Arizona, had escaped him, but he knew he'd find him again. Jacob Payne, soon to be a legend in Arizona, would get his man, whether that be a thousand-dollar bounty, or just a simple, inept forty-dollar outlaw.

Lonesome Trail

Before Jacob Payne arrived in the Arizona Territory, before he was a bounty hunter, before he learned how to survive in the desert, he had to travel west. Innocents in trouble, quirky characters and life-threatening peril are along every mile as he

passed from Virginia through Texas to the desert of Arizona.

When Jacob comes across a family that has

fallen victim to horse thieves, he can't just ride on and leave them to his fate. He's not yet a bounty hunter, but Jacob Payne can still hunt down the evil-doers. Tucson will be waiting for him once he brings these men to justice.

Sign-up to download this prequel story for free from my website:

http://atbutler.com/jp-free

ALSO BY A.T. BUTLER

Jacob Payne Series:

Trouble By Any Name

Danger in the Canyon

Justice for Jasper

Blood on the Mountain

Outlaw Country

Death By Grit

Desert Rage

Arizona Legend

Fool's Demise

Silent Night

Courage On The Oregon Trail Series:

Westward Courage

Faithful Trail

Frontier Sisters

Unyielding Heart

Wild Promise

Fierce Dreams

Other Western Novels by A.T. Butler:

Hawke's Revenge

Loyalty's Price

The next book in the Jacob Payne series, ***Fool's Demise***,

is available now!

ABOUT THE AUTHOR

I grew up in the southwest—California Missions, snakes and constant threat of drought weaving the backdrop of my childhood.

But it wasn't until I moved to Texas a few years ago that the magic and mythology of the American West began to seep into my soul.

I'd love to write about Jacob Payne for a long time...

If you enjoyed this book, a review on your favorite retailer would be greatly appreciated.

- A

Arizona Legend is a work of fiction. Names, characters, places and incidents either are the product of the author's imagination or are used fictitiously. Any resemblance to actual persons living or dead, events or locales is entirely coincidental.

Copyright 2019 by A.T. Butler

All rights reserved.

No part of this publication may be reproduced, distributed, or transmitted in any form or by any means, including photocopying, recording or other electronic or mechanical methods, without the prior written permission of the publisher, except in the case of brief quotations embodied in critical reviews and certain other noncommercial uses permitted by copyright law.

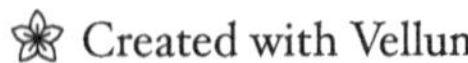 Created with Vellum

www.ingramcontent.com/pod-product-compliance
Lightning Source LLC
Chambersburg PA
CBHW060747210726
48292CB00015B/2821